For Keating, Sagan, Tieren, and Deme

David Hyde Costello is the author and illustrator of *Here They Come!*
He lives in Amherst, Massachusetts.

Copyright © 2010 by David Hyde Costello
All rights reserved
Color separations by Chroma Graphics PTE Ltd.
Printed in China by 1010 Printing International Limited,
North Point, Hong Kong
Designed by Jay Colvin
First edition, 2010
9   10   8

mackids.com

Library of Congress Cataloging-in-Publication Data
Costello, David.
    I can help / David Hyde Costello.— 1st ed.
        p.   cm.
    Summary: When a duck gets lost and a monkey helps him
find his way, it starts a chain reaction in which all the young
animals help each other solve their problems.
    ISBN: 978-0-374-33526-7
    [1. Helpfulness—Fiction.   2. Animals—Fiction.]   I. Title.

PZ7.C8228 Iac 2010
[E]—dc22
                                                    2005044321

Uh-oh. I'm lost.

I can help.

Thank you, monkey!

Uh-oh. I'm falling.

I can help.

Thank you, giraffe!

Uh-oh. I can't reach.

I can help.

Thank you, gorilla!

Uh-oh. I have a splinter.

I can help.

Thank you, sunbird!

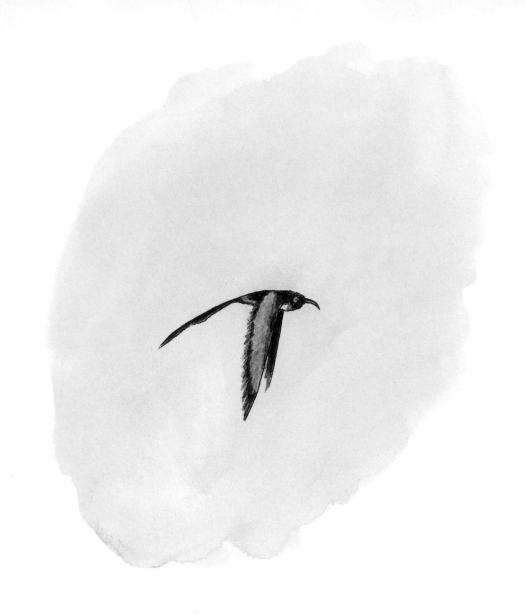

Uh-oh. I'm tired.

I can help.

Thank you, elephant!

Uh-oh. I'm hot and thirsty.

I can help.

Follow me!

Thank you, duck!

You're welcome!

Uh-oh. I'm lost again.

We can help!